JAN BRETT

The SNOWY NAP

G. P. Putnam's Sons

For my grandnephew Tate Merrill Littlehale

G. P. PUTNAM'S SONS
an imprint of Penguin Random House LLC
375 Hudson Street
New York, NY 10014

Library of Congress Cataloging-in-Publication Data
Names: Brett, Jan, 1949– author, illustrator.
Title: The snowy nap / Jan Brett.
Description: New York, NY : G. P. Putnam's Sons, [2018] Summary: After hearing about winter from
his friends, Hedgie the hedgehog tries to stay awake to experience its wonders.
Identifiers: LCCN 2017037742 (print) | LCCN 2017050688 (ebook) | ISBN 9780698174634 (Ebook) |
ISBN 9780698174641 (Ebook) | ISBN 9780399170737 (hardcover)
Subjects: | CYAC: Hedgehogs—Fiction. | Winter—Fiction. | Hibernation—Fiction.
Classification: LCC PZ7.B7559 (ebook) | LCC PZ7.B7559 Sn 2018 (print) | DDC [E]—dc23
LC record available at https://lccn.loc.gov/2017037742

Manufactured in China by RR Donnelley Asia Printing Solutions Ltd.
ISBN 9780399170737
1 3 5 7 9 10 8 6 4 2

Design by Marikka Tamura. Text set in LTC Cloister.
The art for this book was done in watercolors and gouache,
Airbrush backgrounds by Joseph Hearne.

Young Hedgie sniffed the chilly wind. *Snow is on the way,*
he thought. *I'll just take a last ramble around the farm.*
He did not want to miss a moment.

He could barely keep his eyes open as he walked. The hens noticed at once.

"Time for beddy-bye," they cackled. "It won't be long before you have to hibernate and our coop will be bedazzled by icicles."

In a sleepy daze, Hedgie trundled past the pond.
The geese honked, "Good-bye until spring. We'll think of you as
we play slip and slide across the pond ice. It is already starting to freeze."

Hedgie came to the sheep shed.

"Nighty night," the sheep baa-aaed. One of the sheep had seen hedgehogs on the farm head for their cozy dens year after year as winter arrived. She also was ready to tell Hedgie what he would miss.

"I'll soon see the snowmen Lisa makes," she said.

The billy goat overheard and crunched across the frozen field to add, "As usual, you will miss winter blue time, when the sun sets and the snowy farm appears in every shade of blue."

The pig watched Hedgie stop for a big yawn. "Have a good winter's sleep," she oinked. "If only I could save a few snowflakes for you. No two are alike."

When the pony trotted up, Hedgie guessed what he wanted to say. "Sleep well," he neighed. "If you hear bells in your dreams, it will be me pulling my sleigh."

That was the last straw.

"I don't want to sleep all winter like last year," protested Hedgie. "I want to see icicles and snowmen, snowflakes and pond ice. I want to hear sleigh bells."

Before Hedgie could yawn again, he decided to turn around and stay up for the winter.

The night grew frosty cold. "Must stay awake, must stay awake, must stay awake to see winter." Hedgie shivered, and his eyes closed.

From the farmhouse window, Lisa saw a still shape outside in the cold. "Poor little hedgehog is frozen stiff!" she cried. She bundled him up and brought him inside.

Lisa put Hedgie in a tea cozy and gave him a spot by the window.
"That was a close call," she said. "A snowstorm is on the way.
You'd better stay in the house and warm up."

To Hedgie's delight, the next morning he saw the world outside shimmering with snow. The old chicken coop sparkled like a palace.

Every day he watched from different windows
and new wintry scenes appeared.

The pond froze into a shiny mirror. Lisa twirled on her skates
as the goose and the gander slid to keep up.

To Hedgie's amazement, one day Lisa rolled great balls of snow.
Before he knew it, he was looking at his first snowman.
He was getting sleepier, but each morning held a new surprise.

The little hedgehog was dozing when he heard the tinkling of bells. He tried with all his might and opened his eyes.

There was the pony pulling a sleigh. Lisa made a snowball and tossed it in his direction, *Ka-poof!*

Hedgie slept later every day. One day he awoke to see flowers of frost
decorating his window. The trees looked like lace against the sky.
I have truly seen winter was Hedgie's last thought as he nodded back to sleep.

Lisa knew it was time.

Leaving the door ajar, she cradled the little hedgehog. "You belong in the wild," she whispered in his ear as she carried him through the drifts.

She crouched by his burrow and nestled him inside. "Sweet dreams, little adventurer," she said.

Just then, she noticed the front door was swinging on its hinges.
Squawks and rumbles were coming from inside.

Lisa peered through the doorway and saw animals, higgledy-piggledy,
making a commotion in her house.
Each one was thinking, *I'll see winter from a nice warm house.*

"Out, out OUT! Skedaddle!" She laughed.
"Don't you know this is not where you live?"

Lisa was shooing the last mouse from the house as Hedgie, snug in his burrow, fell into a deep sleep. He was dreaming about icicles and snowmen, snowflakes and pond ice. It was a long snowy nap.